W9-BFU-538

WITHDRAWN

Copyright © 2019 by Myrtle Washington Brown. 797391

All rights reserved. No part of this book may
be reproduced or transmitted in any form or by
any means, electronic or mechanical, including
photocopying, recording, or by any information
storage and retrieval system, without permission
in writing from the copyright owner.

This is a work of fiction. Names, characters,
places and incidents either are the product of the
author's imagination or are used fictitiously, and
any resemblance to any actual persons, living or
dead, events, or locales is entirely coincidental.

To order additional copies of this book, contact:
Xlibris
1-888-795-4274
www.Xlibris.com
Orders@Xlibris.com

ISBN: Softcover   978-1-7960-4720-2
       EBook   978-1-7960-4721-9

Print information available on the last page

Rev. date: 07/17/2019

A FRIEND IN NEED
IS
A FRIEND INDEED

Myrtle Washington Brown

Asher was playing basketball with his friend, Isaac, outside his house. He was shooting the ball and making all of his shots. He made sure that he practiced shooting the ball on most days, and it was paying off. He was so excited that he was doing so well. His best friend, Isaac, was giving him high fives.

"Hey guys!" brothers and twins Levi and Seth came over with their basketball. All of the boys knew each other because they all went to the same school. "Asher, you are on fire, man!" Have you missed a shot yet? Seth asked. "Not yet, but don't jinx me. The boys took turns shooting the basketball and Asher finally miss a shot.

They all laughed and went and sat under the big oak tree in the yard. Asher sprawled under the tree as the boys talked about school, girls and all the things boys razz each other about.

Then, the boys noticed that Asher got quiet. "Guys, I have to tell you something. My mom and dad told me and my sister that they're getting a divorce. He became quiet again. No one said anything for a while.

Seth finally said, "Asher, I feel bad for you, but everything's gonna be okay. Your parents will still love you and your sister. I don't know why parents have to leave their family but, sometimes, they do.

The usual happy Isaac looked somber, as well. He said, "I already talked to him about it and told him that I would always be there for him. And if my mom and dad could help him, they will.

Levi was quiet as usual. Asher finally said, "I know that my parents love me and my sister, but it just makes me sad that we won't be together as a family, and that's what I'm gonna miss, us together.

Levi finally spoke up. "I would hate for me and Seth to ever be separated. We have always been there for each other, so I can understand you when you say you would miss being together."

Asher said, "You know it makes me feel better just to talk about it. Just being around my friends who have my back makes me feel better. I know that my mom and dad will always be my mom and dad, and I know that they will still be there for me, but not having them both here as a family really hurts."

Seth said, "You have to tell your parents how you feel and how much it hurts you that they are divorcing. They need to know that. I think once you talk to them about how you feel, you will feel better." "You're right, Asher said, I do need to talk to my parents. It's gonna be scary to me, but I need to do that." Everyone sat quietly for a while. Asher broke the silence, "You know, I just realized that you guys are my family too. So, if I can talk to you I can talk to my parents. And, I'm gonna do it today. Asher stood up and moved toward the basketball goal. "Let's go shoot some more hoops! I was on point!"

The End

Author's note: the meaning of Asher, "happy, blessed", the meaning of Isaac, "to laugh", the meaning of Seth, "appointed, placed" and the meaning of Levi, "attached, joined"

The moral of this story is a good friend can always make difficult and challenging things in life better and good friends are like family.

Printed in the United States
By Bookmasters